My love affair with myths and legends began when my mom, Flossie, read to me and my older brother every single night.

Flossie didn't read the usual fairy tales like "Cinderella" or "Sleeping Beauty." Instead she started with Nathaniel Hawthorne's retelling of the Greek myths. I especially loved "The Pomegranate Seeds"—the Persephone story.

Then on to THE ARABIAN NIGHTS and Ali Baba, my favorite in this exotic world. Imagine my surprise years later when I found out that "open sesame" were not only the magic words, but seeds on my bagel, too!

I wept and wept over my all-time favorite legend, "The Tongue-cut Sparrow," from Japan. It was so sad and I loved it.

As I grew older, my taste veered toward the more comical tales. It was then that I began to realize I could retell legends in my own personal way.

Here is a collection of four of my favorites; three are about wildflowers and one is about bread!

I hope you enjoy them.

♡Tomie

TOMIE DEPAOLA'S BIG BOOK OF FAVORITE LEGENDS

Tomie 2007

Retold and Illustrated by Tomie dePaola

G. P. PUTNAM'S SONS

G. P. PUTNAM'S SONS

A division of Penguin Young Readers Group.

Published by The Penguin Group.

Penguin Group (USA) Inc., 375 Hudson Street, New York, NY 10014, U.S.A.

Penguin Group (Canada), 90 Eglinton Avenue East, Suite 700, Toronto, Ontario M4P 2Y3, Canada (a division of Pearson Penguin Canada Inc.).

Penguin Books Ltd, 80 Strand, London WC2R 0RL, England.

Penguin Ireland, 25 St. Stephen's Green, Dublin 2, Ireland (a division of Penguin Books Ltd.).

Penguin Group (Australia), 250 Camberwell Road, Camberwell, Victoria 3124, Australia (a division of Pearson Australia Group Pty Ltd).

Penguin Books India Pvt Ltd, 11 Community Centre, Panchsheel Park, New Delhi - 110 017, India.

Penguin Group (NZ), 67 Apollo Drive, Rosedale, North Shore 0745, Auckland, New Zealand (a division of Pearson New Zealand Ltd).

Penguin Books (South Africa) (Pty) Ltd, 24 Sturdee Avenue, Rosebank, Johannesburg 2196, South Africa.

Penguin Books Ltd, Registered Offices: 80 Strand, London WC2R 0RL, England.

Published simultaneously in Canada.

Manufactured in China by South China Printing Co. Ltd.

Design by Marikka Tamura and Ryan Thomann.

Library of Congress Cataloging-in-Publication Data available upon request.

ISBN 978-0-399-25035-4

1 3 5 7 9 10 8 6 4 2

First Impression

CONTENTS

THE LEGEND OF
❦ THE BLUEBONNET ❧

AN OLD TALE OF TEXAS

Great Spirits,
the land is dying. Your People are dying, too,"
the long line of dancers sang.
"Tell us what we have done to anger you.
End this drought. Save your People.
Tell us what we must do so you will send the rain
that will bring back life."

For three days,
the dancers danced to the sound of the drums,
and for three days, the People called Comanche
watched and waited.
And even though the hard winter was over,
no healing rains came.

Drought and famine are hardest
on the very young and the very old.

Among the few children left
was a small girl named She-Who-Is-Alone.
She sat by herself watching the dancers.
In her lap was a doll made from buckskin—a warrior doll.
The eyes, nose and mouth were painted on
with the juice of berries. It wore beaded leggings
and a belt of polished bone.
On its head were brilliant blue feathers
from the bird who cries "Jay-jay-jay."
She loved her doll very much.

"Soon," She-Who-Is-Alone said to her doll,
"the shaman will go off alone to the top of the hill
to listen for the words of the Great Spirits.
Then, we will know what to do so that once more
the rains will come and the Earth will be green and alive.
The buffalo will be plentiful
and the People will be rich again."

As she talked, she thought of the mother who made
the doll, of the father who brought the blue feathers.
She thought of the grandfather and the grandmother
she had never known. They were all like shadows.
It seemed long ago that they had died from the famine.
The People had named her and cared for her.
The warrior doll was the only thing she had left
from those distant days.

"The sun is setting," the runner called
as he ran through the camp. "The shaman is returning."
The People gathered in a circle and the shaman spoke.

"I have heard the words of the Great Spirits," he said.
"The People have become selfish.
For years, they have taken from the Earth
without giving anything back.
The Great Spirits say the People must sacrifice.
We must make a burnt offering
of the most valued possession among us.
The ashes of this offering shall then be scattered to
the four points of the Earth, the Home of the Winds.
When this sacrifice is made,
drought and famine will cease.
Life will be restored to the Earth and to the People!"

The People sang a song of thanks to the Great Spirits
for telling them what they must do.

"I'm sure it is not my new bow
that the Great Spirits want," a warrior said.
"Or my special blanket," a woman added,
as everyone went to their tipis to talk and think over
what the Great Spirits had asked.

Everyone, that is, except She-Who-Is-Alone.
She held her doll tightly to her heart.
"You," she said, looking at the doll.
"You are my most valued possession.
It is you the Great Spirits want."
And she knew what she must do.

As the council fires died out
and the tipi flaps began to close,
the small girl returned to the tipi,
where she slept, to wait.

The night outside was still except for the distant sound
of the night bird with the red wings.
Soon everyone in the tipi was asleep, except She-Who-Is-Alone.
Under the ashes of the tipi fire one stick still glowed.
She took it and quietly crept out into the night.

She ran to the place on the hill
where the Great Spirits had spoken to the shaman.
Stars filled the sky, but there was no moon.
"O Great Spirits," She-Who-Is-Alone said,
"here is my warrior doll. It is the only thing I have
from my family who died in this famine.
It is my most valued possession. Please accept it."

Then, gathering twigs,
she started a fire with the glowing firestick.
The small girl watched
as the twigs began to catch and burn.

She thought of her grandmother and grandfather,
her mother and father and all the People—
their suffering, their hunger.
And before she could change her mind,
she thrust the doll into the fire.

She watched until the flames died down
and the ashes had grown cold.
Then, scooping up a handful, She-Who-Is-Alone
scattered the ashes to the Home of the Winds,
the North and the East, the South and the West.

And there she fell asleep
until the first light of the morning sun woke her.

She looked out over the hill,
and stretching out from all sides, where the ashes had fallen,
the ground was covered with flowers—beautiful flowers,
as blue as the feathers in the hair of the doll,
as blue as the feathers of the bird who cries "Jay-jay-jay."

When the People came out of their tipis,
they could scarcely believe their eyes.
They gathered on the hill with She-Who-Is-Alone
to look at the miraculous sight.
There was no doubt about it,
the flowers were a sign of forgiveness
from the Great Spirits.

And as the People sang
and danced their thanks to the Great Spirits,
a warm rain began to fall
and the land began to live again.
From that day on,
the little girl was known by another name—
"One-Who-Dearly-Loved-Her-People."

And every spring,
the Great Spirits remember the sacrifice of a little girl
and fill the hills and valleys of the land, now called Texas,
with the beautiful blue flowers.
Even to this very day.

Author's Note

The bluebonnet is a form of wild lupine. It is known by other names, too, such as Lupine, Buffalo Clover, Wolf Flower, and "El Conejo"—the rabbit. But its most familiar name, Bluebonnet, probably began when the white settlers moved to Texas. The lovely blue flowers they saw growing wild were thought to resemble the bonnets worn by many of the women to shield them from the hot Texas sun.

The suggestion to do a book for children on the origin of the Texas state flower came to me from Margaret Looper, a reading consultant in Huntsville, Texas. Gathering folktale material is always interesting, but more so when the suggestion to "look at" a tale comes from a friend. Margaret sent me a copy and I cannot thank her enough, for I was immediately drawn to it.

Then, with tireless effort, Margaret kept me supplied with as many versions as she could locate; and during one long New Hampshire winter, my mailbox was filled with information and pictures of that lovely spring wildflower.

Margaret also helped me find out about the Comanche People, especially details about their early life in Texas before it became impossible for these brave people to share the land with the settlers and they were expelled or had to flee.

When doing a book based on a legend involving real people, it becomes a drive to find out as much as possible about their customs and way of life in an effort to portray as accurate and full a picture as possible. In this search, one comes upon information that fascinates. One point especially interesting to me was that the Comanche People did not have a concept of one god or a Great Spirit. They worshiped many spirits equally, and each one represented a special skill or trait. They prayed to the Deer Spirit for agility, the Wolf Spirit for ferocity, the Eagle Spirit for strength, and to the important Buffalo Spirit to send them buffalo for the hunt. The Crow Spirit was evil. Therefore, in my retelling, the People pray to the Great Spirits collectively.

Even though the legend of the bluebonnet is a tale about the origin of a flower, for me it is more a tale of the courage and sacrifice of a young person. She-Who-Is-Alone's act of thrusting her beloved doll into the fire to save her people represents the decisive sort of action that many young people are capable of, the kind of selfless action that creates miracles.

TdeP

The Legend of
the Indian Paintbrush

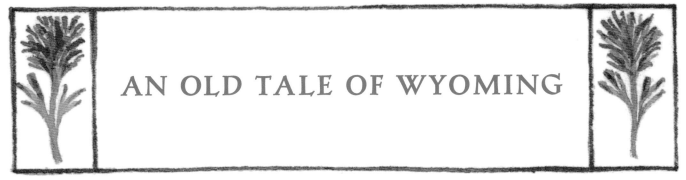

AN OLD TALE OF WYOMING

For my dear friends,
Pat Henry and her husband, Bill,
who shared their part of Wyoming with me
and didn't make me ride a horse.
TdeP

Many years ago
when the People traveled the Plains
and lived in a circle of teepees,
there was a boy who was smaller
than the rest of the children in the tribe.
No matter how hard he tried,
he couldn't keep up with the other boys
who were always riding, running, shooting their bows,
and wrestling to prove their strength.
Sometimes his mother and father worried for him.

But the boy, who was called Little Gopher,
was not without a gift of his own.
From an early age, he made toy warriors
from scraps of leather and pieces of wood
and he loved to decorate smooth stones
with the red juices from berries
he found in the hills.
The wise shaman of the tribe understood
that Little Gopher had a gift that was special.
"Do not struggle, Little Gopher.
Your path will not be the same as the others.
They will grow up to be warriors.
Your place among the People will be remembered
for a different reason."

And in a few years
when Little Gopher was older,
he went out to the hills alone
to think about becoming a man,
for this was the custom of the tribe.
And it was there that a Dream-Vision came to him.

The sky filled with clouds and out of them
came a young Indian maiden and an old grandfather.
She carried a rolled-up animal skin
and he carried a brush made of fine animal hairs
and pots of paints.

The grandfather spoke.
"My son, these are the tools
by which you shall become great among your People.
You will paint pictures of the deeds of the warriors
and the visions of the shaman,
and the People shall see them and remember them forever."

The maiden unrolled a pure white buckskin
and placed it on the ground.
"Find a buckskin as white as this," she told him.
"Keep it and one day you will paint a picture
that is as pure as the colors
in the evening sky."

And as she finished speaking, the clouds cleared
and a sunset of great beauty filled the sky.
Little Gopher looked at the white buckskin
and on it he saw colors as bright and beautiful
as those made by the setting sun.

Then the sun slowly sank behind the hills,
the sky grew dark,
and the Dream-Vision was over.
Little Gopher returned to the circle of the People.

43

The next day he began to make soft brushes
from the hairs of different animals
and stiff brushes from the hair of the horses' tails.
He gathered berries and flowers
and rocks of different colors
and crushed them to make his paints.

He collected the skins of animals,
which the warriors brought home from their hunts.
He stretched the skins on wooden frames
and pulled them until they were tight.

And he began to paint pictures . . .

Of great hunts . . .

Of great deeds . . . .

Of great Dream-Visions . . .
So that the People would always remember.

But even as he painted,
Little Gopher sometimes longed
to put aside his brushes
and ride out with the warriors.
But always he remembered his Dream-Vision
and he did not go with them.

Many months ago,
he had found his pure white buckskin,
but it remained empty
because he could not find the colors of the sunset.
He used the brightest flowers,
the reddest berries,
and the deepest purples from the rocks,
and still his paintings never satisfied him.
They looked dull and dark.

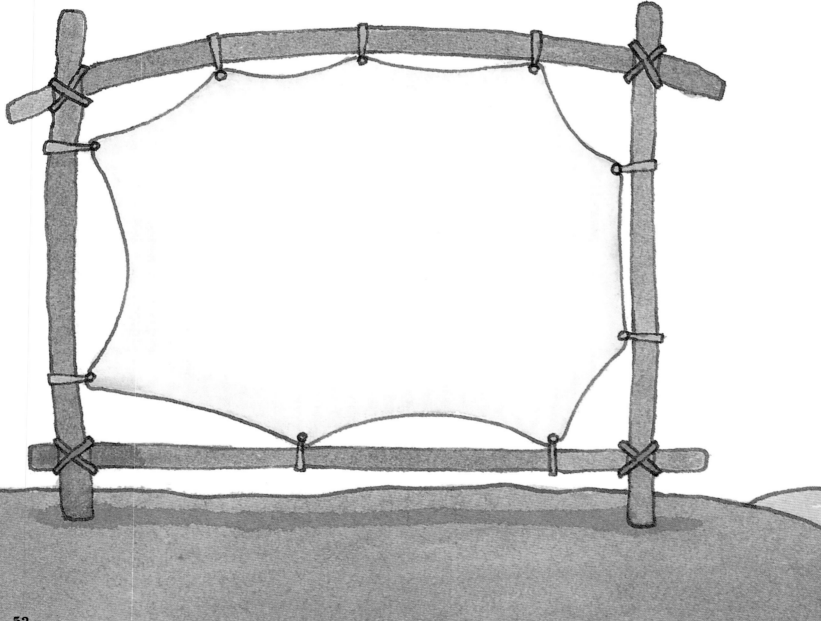

He began to go to the top of a hill each evening
and look at the colors that filled the sky
to try and understand how to make them.
He longed to share the beauty of his Dream-Vision
with the People.

But he never gave up trying,
and every morning when he awoke
he took out his brushes and his pots of paints
and created the stories of the People
with the tools he had.

One night as he lay awake,
he heard a voice calling to him.
"Because you have been faithful to the People
and true to your gift,
you shall find the colors you are seeking.

Tomorrow take the white buckskin
and go to the place
where you watch the sun in the evening.
There on the ground you will find what you need."

The next evening as the sun began to go down,
Little Gopher put aside his brushes
and went to the top of the hill
as the colors of the sunset spread across the sky.

And there, on the ground all around him,
were brushes filled with paint,
each one a color of the sunset.
Little Gopher began to paint quickly and surely,
using one brush, then another.

And as the colors in the sky began to fade,
Little Gopher gazed at the white buckskin
and he was happy.
He had found the colors of the sunset.
He carried his painting down
to the circle of the People,
leaving the brushes on the hillside.

And the next day, when the People awoke,
the hill was ablaze with color,
for the brushes had taken root in the earth
and multiplied into plants
of brilliant reds, oranges and yellows.

And every spring from that time,
the hills and meadows burst into bloom.

And every spring,
the People danced and sang the praises
of Little Gopher who had painted for the People.

And the People no longer called him Little Gopher,
but He-Who-Brought-the-Sunset-to-the-Earth.

Author's Note

The lovely red, orange, yellow (and even pink) Indian Paintbrush blooms in profusion throughout Wyoming, Texas, and the high plains, and has many stories connected with its origin. The story of the Native American artist and his desire to paint the sunset was particularly meaningful to me as an artist. (There are many times when I wish I could go out on a hill and find brushes filled with exactly the colors I need. Who knows . . . someday maybe . . .)

The idea for doing a book on this spectacular wildflower came from my good friend Pat Henry after she had seen my book *The Legend of the Bluebonnet*, which is the story of the Texas state flower. Pat is from Wyoming where the Indian Paintbrush is the state flower.

Coincidentally, Carolyn Sullivan from Austin, Texas, had recently sent me a copy of *Texas Wildflowers, Stories and Legends*, a collection of articles by Ruth D. Isely which originally appeared in the *Austin American-Statesman*. Carolyn is a teacher in the Austin area, and in 1965 this collection was made available to teachers there for use with a unit on Texas trees and wildflowers. She too had read the bluebonnet book and knew of my deep interest in folktale and legend.

The Indian Paintbrush is a familiar flower to Texans and in the book I came across a brief and interesting account of how the wildflower got its name. I contacted Mrs. Isely and she graciously gave me permission to use her article as the main source for my retelling of the legend of the Indian Paintbrush.

So, I would like to thank Pat Henry for suggesting the book, Carolyn Sullivan for sending me the collection of legends and Ruth Isely for giving me inspiration from her collection. I would also like to thank and acknowledge Lady Bird Johnson, the former First Lady, whose untiring efforts have not only made her home state of Texas a symphony of color with its wildflowers, but have encouraged other states throughout the country in the preserving and growing of native wildflowers to beautify the countryside.

TdeP

The Legend of ❊ the Poinsettia ❊

AN OLD TALE OF MEXICO

To Chris O'Brien, who knows
that the beauty of the gift is in the giving.
TdeP

Lucida lived in a small village
high up in the mountains of Mexico
with her mama, her papa,
and her younger brother and sister, Paco and Lupe.
Papa worked in the fields with their burro, Pepito.
Every evening Lucida fed Pepito, gave him fresh water,
and filled his stall with clean straw.

At home Lucida helped Mama
clean their *casita*—their little house—
and pat out the tortillas for their meals.

She took care of Paco and Lupe, and each evening
they went to the shrine of the Virgin of Guadalupe
near the front gate to see if fresh candles were needed.

But every day was not work.
On Sundays the family went to San Gabriel
in the square where Padre Alvarez said the Mass.
And all through the year there were fiestas
and holy days, which always began with a procession
that wound through the village and ended in San Gabriel.

One day, close to Christmas—*la Navidad*—
Padre Alvarez came to their casita.
"Ah, Señora Martinez, *buenos días*—good day,"
Padre Alvarez said. "I am here to ask you about the blanket
which covers the figure of the Baby Jesus
in the Christmas procession.

We have used the same one for so many years
that it is almost worn out.
Because your weaving is so fine, I have come to ask
if you would make a new one."
"*Mi padre*," Lucida's mother said, "I would be honored.
And Lucida will help me."

On Saturday Lucida and Mama went to the market
to buy the wool for the blanket. They chose
the finest yarn they could find.

At home Lucida helped Mama dye the wool
the colors of the rainbow.
"Those colors will shine throughout the church,"
Papa said, as he watched Lucida and Mama
string the yarn on the loom.

As Christmas drew closer,
everyone in the village was busy.
All the mamas were making gifts to place
at the manger of the Baby Jesus in the church.
The papas worked together putting up
the manger scene in San Gabriel.

Lucida and the other children went to the church
for singing practice for the Christmas Eve procession,
when everyone would walk to San Gabriel,
singing and carrying candles.
Once inside, Padre Alvarez would lay
the figure of the Baby Jesus in the manger,
and the villagers would go up
and place their gifts around it.
"Our gift will be the blanket for the Baby Jesus,"
Lucida told her friends. "I am helping Mama weave it."

One afternoon a few days before Christmas Eve,
Lucida and the children were singing in the church
when Señora Gomez came hurrying in.
"Lucida, you must come home. Your mama is sick
and your papa has taken her down to the town
to see the doctor. You must take care of your
brother and sister until your papa returns tonight."
Lucida was frightened. Mama had never been sick before.

When she got home, Paco and Lupe were crying.
They were frightened, too. Lucida tried to comfort them.
She made some food and sat down to wait for Papa.

That evening Papa came in looking tired and worried.
He drew Lucida close and said, "Lucida, *mi niña,*
your mama is ill. Your aunt—Tía Carmen—
will take care of Mama until she is well,
but I must go back and stay with Mama
until I can bring her home.
But it won't be until after Christmas.
Señora Gomez will take care of you and Paco and Lupe
while I am gone. She will come for you tomorrow."

The next afternoon Lucida overheard two women talking.
"Lucida's mama is ill. She won't be able to finish
the blanket for the procession. Isn't it a shame?"
"*Sí*," the other woman said. "We are all so disappointed.
Padre Alvarez will have to use the old worn-out one."

When Lucida went home to feed Pepito
and get clothes for Paco, Lupe, and herself,
she looked at the unfinished blanket on the loom.

Perhaps I can finish it, she thought.
But when she sat down and tried to weave,
the yarn got tangled. The more she tried
to untangle it, the worse it got. It was no use.
She could never finish it by herself.

She took the unfinished blanket to Señora Gomez.
"Oh, Lucida, it is so tangled. There isn't time
for me to fix it," Señora Gomez told her.
"Tomorrow is Christmas Eve."
Lucida started to cry.
It was her fault the blanket was ruined.

Her family wouldn't have a gift
to place at the manger of the Baby Jesus.
"Don't worry, Lucida. We will all go
to the procession together."
Lucida didn't say anything, but in her heart
she felt that she had ruined Christmas.

"Come, Paco; come, Lupe. It is time to go to the procession,"
Señora Gomez called on Christmas Eve. "Where is Lucida?"
She was nowhere to be found. Lucida was hiding.

From the shadows, Lucida watched everyone gather
for the procession. The candles were lit, the singing began,
and the villagers walked to San Gabriel,
carrying gifts to place at the manger.
Lucida walked along in the darkness
and watched the procession go into the church,
followed by Padre Alvarez carrying the Baby Jesus.

"Little girl, are you Lucida?" An old woman
stood in the shadows nearby.
"Sí," Lucida answered, wondering who she was.
"I have a message for you. Your mama is going to be fine,
and your papa will bring her home soon.
So you don't have to worry.
Go now into the church and celebrate Christmas
with the others. Paco and Lupe are waiting for you."

90

"I can't," Lucida told her. "I don't have a gift
  for the Baby Jesus.
  Mama and I were weaving a beautiful blanket,
  but I couldn't finish it.
  I tried, but I only tangled it all up."
"Ah, Lucida, any gift is beautiful because it is given,"
  the old woman told her. "Whatever you give, the Baby Jesus
  will love, because it comes from you."
"But what can I give now?" Lucida said, looking around.

A patch of tall green weeds grew in a tangle nearby.
Lucida rushed over and picked an armful.
"Do you think these will be all right?" Lucida turned
to ask the old woman, but she was gone.

Lucida walked into the church. It was blazing
with candlelight, and the children were singing
as she walked quietly down the aisle
with a bundle of green weeds in her arms.

"What is Lucida carrying?" a woman whispered.
"Why is she bringing weeds into the church?"
     another one murmured.
     Lucida reached the manger scene. She placed the green weeds
around the stable. Then she lowered her head and prayed.

A hush fell over the church. Voices began to whisper.
"Look! Look at the weeds!"
Lucida opened her eyes and looked up.

Each weed was tipped with a flaming red star.
The manger glowed and shimmered
as if lit by a hundred candles.

When everyone went outside after the Mass,
all the clumps of tall green weeds
throughout the town were shining with red stars.
Lucida's simple gift had indeed become beautiful.

And every Christmas to this day, the red stars shine on top of green branches in Mexico. The people call the plants *la Flor de Nochebuena*— the Flower of the Holy Night—the poinsettia.

Author's Note

When I first heard the Mexican legend of the poinsettia, about a little girl who offers weeds to the Christ Child as her gift for Christmas, I was touched by it as only Christmas can touch me. I knew that one day I wanted to create the story in pictures for children.

This lovely Mexican wildflower is known by many names in Mexico: *flor de fuego* (fire flower), *flor de Navidad* (Christmas flower), and *flor de la Nochebuena* (flower of the Holy Night), the name I have used in my story.

The poinsettia found its way to the United States through Dr. Joel Roberts Poinsett, who served as our nation's minister to Mexico from 1825 to 1830. He was fascinated with its beauty and called the plant "painted leaves," because the part often thought of as the flower actually consists of leaves surrounding a smaller flower portion. He took cuttings home with him to South Carolina when he returned from Mexico in 1830.

The Christmas plant, which we call poinsettia after Dr. Poinsett, found its way into our own Christmas traditions, and nothing seems to say "Merry Christmas" better than a beautiful red and green poinsettia.

TdeP

Tony's Bread

AN OLD TALE OF ITALY

For *Lon Driggers* and *Bob Sass,*
who sat there and listened
while I told them this story
TdeP

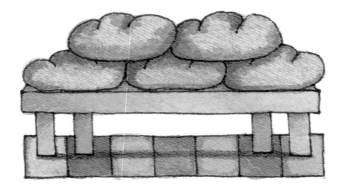

Once, a long time ago, in a small village outside the grand city of Milano, there lived a baker named Antonio. But everyone called him Tony.

Tony made bread and only bread in his bakery. It was good and simple and the villagers loved it. But Tony had a dream. One day he would have a bakery of his own in Milano and become the most famous baker in all of northern Italy.

Now, Tony lived with his only daughter, Serafina. He was a widower and he had raised Serafina from the time she was *una piccola bambina*—a little girl. And how he had spoiled her!

"Antonio treats Serafina like *una principessa*"—a princess— said Zia Clotilda.

"The finest clothes, the finest jewelry, anything her heart desires," said Zia Caterina.

"She never has to lift a finger. All she does is sit, looking out the window eating *dolci*"—sweets—said Zia Clorinda.

"Now that she is old enough to marry, Tony thinks that no man is good enough for his Serafina," the three sisters whispered to each other.

That *was* true. Tony did think that no man was worthy of his darling daughter. He would not even talk to the young men in the village who wanted to court Serafina.

So, poor Serafina would sit at the window behind the curtains, eating her *dolci* and crying.

One day, Angelo, a wealthy nobleman from Milano, was passing through the village. As he went by Tony's house, the wind blew the curtains away from the window, and there sat Serafina. Angelo and Serafina looked into each other's eyes and it was love at first sight for both of them.

The three sisters were standing nearby. "Dear ladies,"
Angelo asked them, "who is that lovely creature sitting at that
window? *Che bella donna!* — What a beautiful woman! Is she
married or spoken for?"

"Ah, young *signore,*" said Zia Clotilda. "That is Serafina, the daughter of Tony the baker. No, she is not married."

"And not likely to be for a long time," said Zia Caterina.

"No one is good enough for Tony's little Serafina," Zia Clorinda explained.

"Well, we'll see about that," said Angelo. "Now, aunties, tell me all you can about her."

The young nobleman and the three sisters sat and talked and talked and talked. And before long, Angelo knew all about Serafina and Tony the baker. And he knew all about Tony's dream of becoming the most famous baker in all of northern Italy.

"*Grazie,* aunties"—thank you—said Angelo. "I think I have a plan that will give Tony his dream and give me the wife of my dreams. But I will need your help. This is what I want you to do…."

The next day, a letter arrived at the bakery for Tony

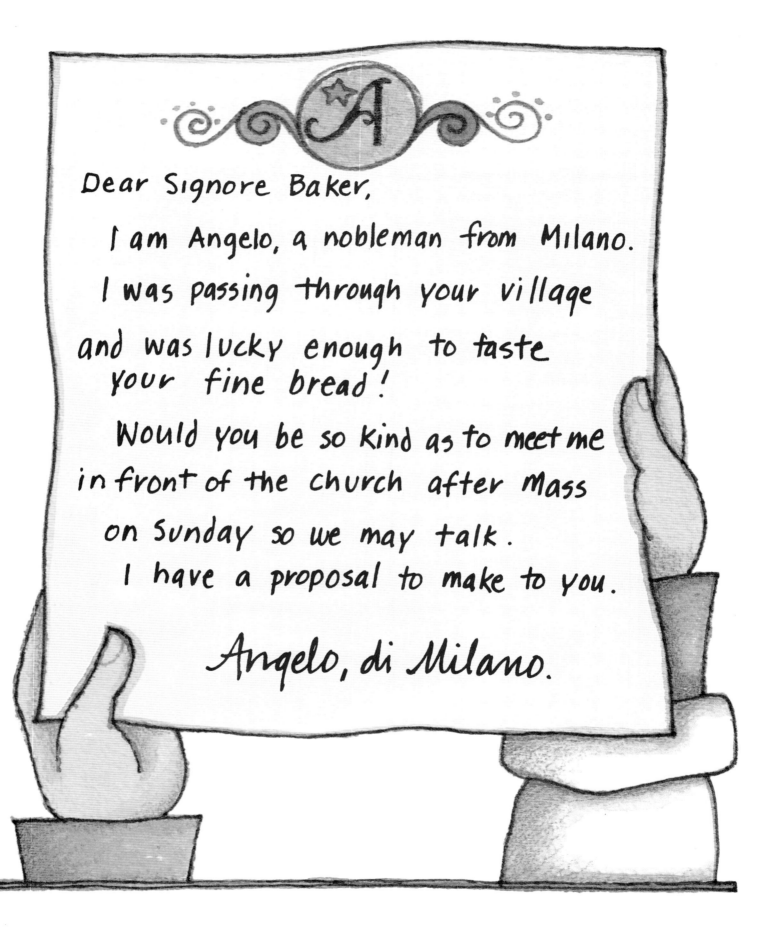

Dear Signore Baker,

I am Angelo, a nobleman from Milano.

I was passing through your village

and was lucky enough to taste your fine bread!

Would you be so kind as to meet me in front of the church after Mass on Sunday so we may talk.

I have a proposal to make to you.

Angelo, di Milano.

and a secret letter arrived at Tony's house for Serafina.

Dear Bella Serafina, ♡ ♡ ♡

I saw you at your window and I love you!

Here's a ring to keep as a symbol of my adoration.

It will not be long before we are HUSBAND and WIFE!

♡ Angelo, your true love.

And Zia Clotilda, Zia Caterina and Zia Clorinda did their part.

"Oh, Tony, did you see that rich young man from Milano?" Zia Clotilda asked.

"He wanted to know all about you. It seems he just loved your bread!" said Zia Caterina.

"Nothing like it in all Milano, he said," Zia Clorinda told Tony. "Why, I wouldn't be surprised if he wanted to meet you, the way he went on."

"Well, dear ladies, funny you should say that, because he does want to meet me—after Mass on Sunday," said Tony. "His name is Angelo di Milano."

"Imagine that!" the three women exclaimed. *"Che bella fortuna"*—What good luck for you. "And for Serafina!" they whispered to each other.

"And so, Signor Antonio, I would be most pleased if
you and your lovely daughter would come to Milano
as my guests," Angelo said.

"And if you like our city, I would be proud to set you up
in a fine bakery of your own near the Piazza del Duomo—
the cathedral square. Your fame would be assured, Signor
Antonio. I will see to that."

Tony couldn't believe his ears. His dream was about to
come true. "Why, thank you, Signor Angelo. But please,
call me Tony. All my friends do."

"Also, Signor Tony," Angelo continued. "The advantages for your beautiful daughter would be great. I admit I would not find it unpleasant for Serafina to sit beside me at my great table as my wife—the daughter of Tony, the most famous baker of Milano."

That did it! Tony agreed, and off he and Serafina went with Angelo. Together they walked all the small streets around the cathedral square and visited all the bakeries and pastry shops.

They tasted *torta*—cake—and *biscotti*—cookies—and *pane*—bread. And Tony was depressed. The bread alone was like nothing Tony had ever tasted: bread made out of the finest, whitest flour; bread shaped like pinwheels; bread with seeds of all sorts scattered over the top.

"It is no use, Signor Angelo," said a very sad Tony. "I can never compete with all these fine bakeries and pastry shops. All I can make is bread, and very simple bread at that. I would be the laughingstock of Milano. It is better if Serafina and I just go home."

"No, never!" Angelo shouted.

"Oh, Papa, no," Serafina cried. Not only was she in love
with Angelo, but she was looking forward to living in that
grand house with all those good things to eat.

"If only you could make bread that tasted as good and sweet as this candied fruit and these raisins," Serafina said.

"Or," Angelo said, getting another idea, "as rich and sweet as this cup of punch made from milk and eggs and honey!"

"Milk, eggs, honey," Tony said, thinking out loud.

"Candied fruit," Serafina said. "Raisins," Angelo chimed in.

"That's it!" all three shouted.

"I shall make the richest, lightest, most wonderful bread anyone has ever tasted—out of the whitest flour, the biggest eggs, the creamiest milk, the sweetest candied fruit and the plumpest raisins," Tony shouted.

"Oh, Papa," Serafina cried, kissing her father.

"Servants," Angelo called, and he sent them off to buy all the fine ingredients Tony would need.

The next morning, Tony, Serafina and all the supplies headed back to the little village.

And Tony began to work. Day after day he experimented until he had mixed the lightest, richest dough with as many raisins and as much candied fruit as he could put into it.

Now he was ready to bake. He sent word to Angelo in Milano that he should come to the bakery the next afternoon. Then he set out the dough in large bowls and went to bed. As Tony slept, the dough began to rise and rise and rise.

The next morning he filled every pan in his shop. One piece of dough was left over so he threw it in a flowerpot and baked it too.

When Angelo arrived, the bread was just coming out of the oven. Everyone held his breath and waited while Tony cut a slice of his new bread. Angelo tasted it. Serafina tasted it. Tony tasted it. Zia Clotilda, Zia Caterina, Zia Clorinda all tasted it.

"That's it!" they shouted.

"I'll take these loaves back to Milano to see what my friends say," Angelo said, and off he went.

In just a few days a letter and a large cart filled with ingredients arrived in the village.

Dear Tony,
   Here are more supplies,
Make as much bread as you can,
and send it to me.
   Then, when I send for you,
I promise you will enter Milano
with flags flying and Serafina
will be mine.
     Your future son-in-law,
       Angelo

P.S.
Please bake all the loaves in flowerpots.
My friends like the shape of that
loaf the best.

Just before Christmas, Angelo sent for Tony and Serafina.
Sure enough, when their coach entered Milano, crowds were
cheering and flags were flying.

"*Benvenuto, Tonio!*"—Welcome, Tony!—the crowds cheered.
"*Benvenuto!*"

The bishop and the mayor were there to greet Tony and Serafina.

"And," said the mayor, "Milano is so happy to have you here, so we may always have enough of your wonderful bread!"

The next day when the bakery door was opened, the bishop's guards were called to keep order. All of Milano was there, except for Serafina and Angelo, who were being married quietly in a small chapel in the cathedral.

All during the wedding, they could hear the crowds cheering, calling for *pan di Tonio*—Tony's bread. And to this day, the *panettone* of Milano is eaten and enjoyed, especially at Christmas.

BRAVA SERAFINA, BRAVO ANGELO.
BRAVO TONY!

Author's Note

Who can resist the wonderful taste of the Italian bread *panettone*? Made with eggs, raisins and candied fruit, this cakelike bread has a strong association with the northern Italian city of Milan. And especially with the *Café Motta* situated across from the cathedral—the *Duomo*—in the world-famous *Galleria*, the elegant glass-enclosed shopping arcade where the Milanese promenade on Sunday afternoons.

Every Christmas, *Motta* sends boatloads of *panettone* to the United States so Americans can enjoy it along with their Milanese counterparts.

Like any good and unique food, *panettone* has several stories explaining its creation. The one that captured my imagination concerns a baker, his daughter and a rich young man. I have taken great liberties in this tale, except for the three wise *zie*—aunties. Everyone who knows anything about the Italians will recognize the three ladies in black who are so inseparable that they form a single silhouette.

TdeP

Tomie dePaola was born in Meriden, Connecticut, in 1934 of Irish and Italian parents. He began to draw before starting school, and he told his family that when he grew up he wanted to "sing and tap dance on the stage and write and draw pictures for children." After receiving his MFA from the California College of Arts and Crafts in Oakland, California, he spent years teaching, painting church murals, and designing greeting cards and stage sets. In 1964 he was offered the opportunity to illustrate his first children's book, *Sound* by Lisa Miller. Gradually he freed himself of other obligations and began to write and illustrate children's books full-time.

Fra Angelico and Giotto, Georges Rouault and Ben Shahn influenced his unique style. DePaola has been the recipient of many prestigious awards, including the Smithson Medal from the Smithsonian Institution, the Kerlan Award from the University of Minnesota for his "singular attainment in children's literature," and the Regina Medal from the Catholic Library Association. In 1976 *Strega Nona* was named a Caldecott Honor Book, and in 1990 dePaola was the United States nominee for the Hans Christian Andersen Award for Illustration. In 2000, *26 Fairmount Avenue* was awarded a Newbery Honor.

Tomie dePaola has illustrated more than 200 children's books, many of which have been published in fifteen countries around the world. He remains one of the most popular creators of books for children and receives more than 100,000 fan letters each year. He (and his Airedale, Brontë) lives in New Hampshire, where his studio is housed in a renovated 200-year-old barn.